AF595549

THE BOOK

There is an exciting opportunity waiting for you out there, a little voice inside Christiana whispers. *Leave your comfort zone and find it.* So she takes the risk, quits her job in Germany and moves to Toronto for a six month sabbatical. The vibrant city welcomes her with candid cordiality. While exploring the many neighborhoods, looking for a purpose, she finds new friends in David and his diverse clique. Unexpected possibilities develop. But how is she to know which one offers the chance of a lifetime?

THE AUTHOR

Alice N. York was born and raised near Munich, Germany. Following her profound hunger for all things technical, she studied industrial and production engineering, and took on the challenge of playing the game.

Before starting her second career as a writer she travelled the world and worked in several sales and marketing positions in technological industries. Now she has remembered her roots and is following her heart. It still tells her: Nothing ventured, nothing gained.

Alice currently lives just outside of Munich near the Alps.

Alice N. York

THE CHANCE

SHORT NOVEL

Translated by

Niall Sellar

CAPSCOVIL | GLONN | GERMANY

German edition published as
„DIE CHANCE“
by CAPSCOVIL Verlag, Glonn
www.capscovil.com

English Edition 07/2022
Perfect Paperback

Cover design: CAPSCOVIL
Cover picture: CAPSCOVIL
Satz: CAPSCOVIL
ISBN 978-3-942358-62-0

For all Torontonians, who welcome strangers to their city with candid cordiality

1

Christiana woke up soaked in sweat. Normally, she was not prone to nightmares. But her subconscious noticed the tension slowly building with each trip to the mailbox. Yoga and a refreshing shower chased away the memories of Rome. Back then, apart from a little cash, she had had everything she needed on her mobile phone, from a plane ticket to the access code for the apartment, and a payment app. All had worked well. Until the phone was stolen from her. Then the odyssey began. That wouldn't happen to her again. She went to the mailbox. Was today the day?

Finally. Christiana dropped the rest of the mail on the kitchen table and concentrated on one envelope. She'd been waiting days for this. Hoping every morning to be able to start planning and book the flight. Thanks to dynamic pricing and increasingly sophisticated algorithms, ticket prices could change significantly from one day to the next.

Such uncertainties made the strategist in her nervous. She liked to do everything that could be done immediately, preferably on the spot. At the moment, the direct flight from Munich to Toronto was still comparatively cheap, and every cent she saved would help her with the next six months. But that could change quickly. Expensive rebooking or cancellation fees would be an enormous burden.

She wanted this direct flight. Not only because it was the most convenient, but also because a stop-over in another foreign city could cause complications. Although she was born and raised in Munich, Christiana had no German citizenship. She was stateless. Her parents came from West

Africa and had escaped with nothing but the clothes on their backs when the bombs and bullets destroyed their home. They had found asylum in Germany. That had been almost three decades ago.

But the documents her parents had taken with them on the run were not enough. They could not prove Christiana's identity at birth to the standard required for the issue of a German passport. That was why Christiana had only received a so-called passport substitute and later a travel document for foreigners. In addition, she had her identity digitally verified via the platform of a start-up company. All that had been needed was a photo and travel document, taken live with her laptop camera. All her data was stored in a blockchain for protection.

Only she had control over which companies or institutions could access her digital identity, which proved she was a real person and not a bot. No one else could use it. When she was travelling outside Europe, she still got a visa to minimize difficulties at immigration. Had it arrived at last?

Christiana opened the envelope from the Canadian Visa Applications Office. As a stateless person, she had to fly to Berlin and have her biometric data recorded on site. It seemed the digital transformation arrived in different places at different times. But the hassle had been worth it.

Many of her friends had taken time out after school or university to see the world. She had never been on the road for more than three weeks, meaning she was looking forward to the six months in Toronto all the more.

Time to form new impressions and gain clarity on some things. She loved her job and no one on the team was prejudiced against her. Deciding to take a sabbatical had not been easy for her. Fortunately, she had been shown a lot of understanding and the promise that there would always be a place for her when she returned. After all, there was a strong link between her employer's industry and her destination. That was comforting.

She had saved up a financial cushion over the last few years that would still give her some security when the six months came to an end. Her charitable work also filled her with real satisfaction. Even if she knew she could get back on board at any time, deep inside there was a little voice that whispered there was more for her to do.

Christiana had thought long and hard about where she wanted to go to follow that voice. She loved Tenerife, especially its nature, and had spent her first holiday exploring the large Spanish island all by herself. But Europe was not far enough away from home. Besides, she knew she would miss the hustle and bustle of a big city.

New York, Chicago or San Francisco, indeed the whole USA, were out of the question at the moment. Even if the country and its nature had a lot to offer. Asia had been tempting. Especially seeing the pictures of her friend Barbara, who had recently moved to Singapore to found her own company in a startup incubator.

In the end, two aspects had been crucial for Christiana's choice: Toronto was considered a role model in terms of diversity and had made its mark in the film industry in recent years. With its many different neighborhoods, the city had so much to offer and there was nature all around. It was also said that the city had a very European character. A good mix, then. Relieved, she booked the flight and applied the visa sticker to her travel document. Then she called Monika. Her friend would move into the apartment while she was away.

2

The big day came faster than expected. Wasn't that always the way? There was a lot to prepare and arrange. The search for an apartment had taken the longest. There was a wide choice, just not in the price range that her budget allowed. Thanks to her persistent search she had finally found one in a central location.

The decision about what to take was made quickly. She was neither a high-heel heroine nor a glitz girl. Finding out about the city was pure joy. Curiosity and anticipation grew with every new piece of information.

In the last few days, she had cooked tons of pasta. One farewell dinner followed the next: with work colleagues, at her church, with her spinning course from the fitness club, and with her family and closest friends. On the last evening, Monika and the TEDxTUM team had organized a surprise party for her. For a change it was a pizza party.

Now Christiana sat in the plane and calmed her nerves with a gin and tonic. The horror of a few minutes ago played over in her mind again and again. After she had checked in her suitcases, she had gone outside to the beer garden. To enjoy some sun before the eight-hour long flight. She paid and was about to leave, when suddenly an older man collapsed at the table next to her.

Without hesitation, she supported him so that he did not hit the ground. A group of men at the next table also jumped in and helped put the man on a bench, feet up. She talked to the man, asked questions so that he would not lose consciousness. His face was as white as a sheet and his reactions slow. Someone called 911. The airport's shift manager came and had the incident described to him. Did the man have a stroke? A circulatory collapse? It was hard to tell.

Christiana had her eyes on the clock. Time was running out. She still had to go through passport control. With many intercontinental flights around this time there could be long queues. Boarding would start in ten minutes. But she wouldn't leave until the paramedics arrived. It didn't seem right to her. Slowly the man's face began to regain color. He smiled at her. "I am an optimist, but with a pretty and helpful woman like you, I don't mind contemplating the dark side," he joked embarrassed.

Finally, the ambulance arrived. She told them what had happened and said goodbye. She really could not wait any longer. Neither would her flight. In the terminal her name was called out for the second time.

Slowly her inner excitement subsided. She had done everything possible. She was sure the man had been close to fainting and was better now. Christiana set her wristwatch back six hours as she made herself comfortable. Karma, she thought, smiling.

Her breathless explanation for almost missing her flight had made an impression. One of the flight attendants had thought she deserved a reward and upgraded her seat to business class. All snuggled up under a cozy blanket, she thought about what to read now. Travel guide or novel? She already had a plan for her first weekend in the city. She chose the latter.

The book promised to be an exciting case study on diversity in the technology sector. The title had caught her eye as she also loved to play games. Tearjerkers weren't really her thing anyway. Just before landing she closed the book.

Stunned at times, she had followed the path of the main character. Page by page, gaining in speed all the time – until the bitter end. There had been many faint signals that hinted at how the novel would end. She wondered. How much truth was there really in the story? You wouldn't wish such an experience on anyone.

3

Upon arrival, Christiana already knew she had made the right choice. No queues at passport control. The welcome of the officer on duty almost warm. He was pleased that she had chosen his city for her longer stay. Both suitcases arrived, undamaged. Airport personnel looked her in the eye, no one turned away in embarrassment. Everywhere she went she was greeted with a friendly hello.

At the taxi stand in front of the terminal people stood patiently in the warm evening sun. Spring had finally arrived, her driver told her, full of happiness. The winters were colder than in Munich. That was why she hadn't flown until May. During the half-hour drive into the city – the opposite lane was crowded with rush hour traffic – the landmark of the city could be seen glowing red from afar in the early evening light.

Her one-room apartment was located in a side street very close to the CN Tower. The key was stored in a number-locked box and made the check-in stress-free. Both large suitcases fitted easily into the elevator, which took her to the ninth floor.

The apartment was surprisingly bright due to the large, ceiling-high balcony window opposite the entrance. On the right was a kitchenette and a high table with bar chairs. In the middle, next to the balcony door, was a comfortable looking sofa. On the left was the bed, separated from the living room by half a wall. This meant that no one in the opposite buildings could watch her sleep. Only when cooking and only with binoculars. Unless she drew the curtains. The bathroom was not huge, but it was big enough. There was even a washing machine and dryer. It was perfect.

She quickly sent a few messages to her family and closest friends to say that she had arrived safely. Many smileys and hearts came back. Monika was happy for her and wrote that she had also settled in well. Christiana thought she would unpack tomorrow. Her legs begged for movement after the long flight. Before the shops closed, she wanted to get a few things for breakfast.

Five minutes later she turned into King Street. Cozy bars and restaurants alternated with small shops, stores and coffee shops. No high-rise buildings cast shadows. Many of the brick or wooden facades were reminiscent of an English small town. A few blocks down, she found a shop that was a cross-between a drugstore and supermarket. The cashier was quite taken with her reusable cotton bag and wished her a nice evening.

Which it was, Christiana thought as she slipped into bed tired and content.

4

The elevator door was open. “Good morning! I heard your door and thought I would wait for you,” a young black man with a baritone voice greeted her, smiling. How often had something like this happened to her in Germany? He had piled up his long black braids into a bun at the top of his head so that he looked almost two heads taller than her. The ends of his braids bobbed up and down with each word.

David, as he introduced himself, had only recently arrived in town and was on his way to the gym. Which he jogged to! He preferred to leave in the morning before the studio became too busy. They also had a spinning session, he confirmed to her.

“Just come along,” he said spontaneously. “I’ll take care of you.” But Christiana already had an idea how she wanted to spend her first day, and a well-known market in a brick building was top of the list.

“Then I’ll just see you for lunch at the St. Lawrence market. Good as well,” he laughed. She looked at him in surprise. How did he know that? But David had already put on his headphones and ran off.

Just around the corner behind the tiny park she saw a small café. The owner watered the flowers outside on the stairs. “What a beautiful day,” she beamed.

Christiana did not need any more invitation to have her bamboo coffee cup filled with cappuccino here. She loved small restaurants where people cooked and worked with all their heart. After the first bite of juicy cake her taste buds immediately confirmed that it was also true for this place.

Arriving at King Street, she turned east. Saturday seemed to be gym day in Toronto. Of the few people on the street, almost all wore sportswear. A few meters on, between the pavement and the rails on which a red and white tram passed by silently every few minutes, wooden chairs in gay colors invited pedestrians to take a short break. But the coffee and her plan to see as much as possible carried her on.

The next thing she noticed was a shop that had something to do with food. It was too early for lunch. But her curiosity was piqued and she took a photo as a reminder. After the next intersection, one restaurant followed the next. Creative names alternated with funny house facades. A certain Fred was obviously not here. Rooftop terraces promised meals at somewhat loftier heights.

With each step, the reflecting glass walls of high-rise buildings grew larger in the background. The culinary mile was followed by an art installation that paid tribute to black women of pop culture. Blurred photos of singers such as Nina Simone or Josephine Baker illustrated the danger that their achievements might fade away. Quite in contrast to those of white, generally male artists, who had more often than not been inspired by their successful black colleagues.

Christiana let herself bask in the captivating charisma of these heroines. The melody of "Feeling Good" swung gently in her head and left her lips as a soft humming. She wanted to sing out loud. At the thought of her friends, with whom she had often sung at weddings, she went on exhilarated. Only to come to an abrupt halt shortly afterwards.

The Canadian Walk of Fame started in front of her on the sidewalk. The stars, or rather maple leaves in the shape of stars, were dedicated to influential people – either locals or people who had lived in Canada for a long time – from film, music, culture and sports. She knew many of the names, but would not have associated them all with this country.

Shania Twain, Céline Dion and Bryan Adams were obvious. Michael J. Fox, Kim Cattrall, Kiefer Sutherland and his father, Corey Hart, Nelly Furtado or Sarah McLachlan not necessarily. Pamela Anderson? The Baywatch mermaid? She wasn't from California?

5

The wind had picked up. Despite the sun it was cooler now. In front of her was a shady gorge formed by the high-rise buildings of the financial sector. In stark contrast to the brightly polished, flower-framed bronze statues in front of an entrance, she saw someone lying homeless on the sidewalk next to the traffic lights; above the air shaft of the subway, whose ascending heat was certainly the reason for the choice of location.

Christiana could not tell whether it was a woman or a man. The entire body was firmly hidden under a blanket. It was as if she could feel the person's shame. She threw some coins into the cardboard box. Deep in thought she continued on.

As if to dispel her dash of sadness, the sun suddenly shone directly on her face. A passage opened up between the towering houses. At its end she saw a green meadow.

Something was on it. She moved closer. It was a herd of bronze cows. Turning back towards King Street a staircase led down. But not to a subway station.

"Path" shone in colorful letters on a post. An underground tunnel network in the center of the city that protected pedestrians from wind and weather and spanned more than 30 kilometers. The first turn of the shovel had been made in 1900. Each color of the individual letters stood for a cardinal point. According to the Guinness Book of World Records, there was currently no larger system of underground passages than this. But the day was too gorgeous to go underground.

She moved on quickly. The financial district was not on her list of preferred places today. What's more, her hunger was slowly returning. She turned into a side street. There was a construction site in front of her. Not quite sure if she had taken the right turn, Christiana approached a young woman.

"I'm sorry. Am I in the right place? I want to go to St. Lawrence Market." The woman beamed at her. "Hey cool! Yeah, it's not far. Just turn left there, then straight ahead and turn right at the next crossing. You will see it at once." Helpfulness was apparently very high on the Torontonians' list of priorities.

The brick building was full of activity. Stands with fresh fruit and vegetables lined up next to long meat counters. Cheese and spices alternated with fragrant bread and raw fish on ice. Appetizing smells of freshly cooked food stimulated her senses from all sides. Although the corridors were full of people, there was no crowd in front of the stands. Couples with prams were respectfully let through. Many seemed to come here regularly and buy from their trusted marketeer. The prices were no more expensive than in the supermarket last night.

After she had been around for a second time, she still did not know what she wanted to eat. What did she fancy? A burrito? Salad? Pork loin in cornmeal? The latter was advertised as a local specialty.

"Hey sunshine," a familiar-sounding voice shouted suddenly. "Welcome to foodie heaven – or hell of decisions. Depending on how you take it." Her elevator encounter from this morning stood behind her laughing.

"Come, I'll buy you some oysters. Then we're going to get a crab cake." Sometimes it was good when someone else made the decisions.

In disbelief she stood in front of the fish counter. There were countless varieties of oysters. Each with a more or less appetizing name. Most of them came from the east coast, the seller explained. But they also had some from the west coast. Those were Gigas, especially big ones. Out of curiosity, she chose one Raspberry Point, one Fiddler's Cove and one Mystic, each because of their names.

David chose a Macintosh and two Gigas: a Beach Angels and a Fat Bastard, the seller approving his choice with a wink. Christiana laughed heartily. She learned that David had come to the city from Berlin two weeks ago and was working on a new business idea. He described himself as someone who could "hack" anything – in a positive sense.

"Then you're an ethical hacker?" asked Christiana after she had sipped the first oyster. "Not really. I'm an engineer and I like to build things." It was important to him to consider the social impact of his work. The incubator at the city's largest university had launched a new program – especially for black founders.

His application had been accepted and, over the next

few months, he would write vast amounts of code, solder components to boards and develop an adaptive transport robot to be produced in small series. Somehow, he was not yet completely satisfied with the first draft of the product.

There was a promisingly large market for it, and not only on paper. Consumers became increasingly lazy when shopping. Potential corporate customers had confirmed there was great demand in interviews. Otherwise he would not have been accepted in the incubator for the so-called sandbox program – for founders who were just starting up. But, in his gut, he still wasn't sure if a transport robot really was the right thing for him.

"Or the fat bastard and the beach angels don't get along," she joked. "But seriously. I'm sure your solution will come at the right time. People are ordering more and more over the internet and the parcel services are almost unable to cope. Still, the thought of four-legged robots running around next to me on the sidewalks or stairwell is quite funny. How did you come to love those dogs?" Christiana wanted to know.

David laughed. "There are already some prototypes out there. Many have wheels and only work on straight paths. Pilot projects are being run in Houston, Phoenix and San Francisco, for example. In Ann Arbor there is now another one with a kind of tricycle. One solution on legs comes from a company I do not ever want to work for. They're too creepy for me," he shuddered. "There's another firm with a similar design and I might be able to get in. Hopefully not just to help them fulfill their BAME quota," he added with a raised eyebrow. "But to be honest I'd rather start something on my own with like-minded people."

The day when driverless vehicles became the standard

for delivering parcels and pizza was not too far in the future in some parts of the world. Logistics solutions held a lot of promise.

The countries with the largest share of online trade were China, USA, Great Britain and Japan – with annual growth rates of 10 to 25 percent. Germany was more moderate at around five percent, but there alone a total of 4.3 billion shipments per year were expected by 2022.

The parcel services were already overloaded and personnel difficult to find. No wonder. The major trading platforms had used their market power to impose extremely low prices on logistic service providers. That had got David thinking.

Most likely, solutions like his would make the already large companies even larger. Still, the technical challenge, especially with regard to safety, was hard to resist. On the last mile, there were even more details to consider than with autonomous cars on roads.

The robots had to be able to communicate with the larger delivery vehicles that brought the parcels from the logistics centers to the individual city districts. Once this was solved, the next hurdle presented itself: safe delivery to the consumer. Every entrance was different. Inside buildings there were either stairs or an elevator that needed to be operated. Backyards could be tricky. Passers-by had to be evaded. Accidents were a major risk, and avoiding them crucial for the solution being accepted.

"I'm sure you won't be bored," nodded Christiana. „Bored? Never heard of it," winked David. „But enough about me. What brings you to Toronto?"

While they strolled to the next fish stall, she told him about her sabbatical, and that she wanted to get a few things straight. Not her whole life story. They knew each other too little for that. She wasn't looking for a flirt, either. Fortunately, neither, as far as she could tell, was he. After taking a last bite of crab cake, he said goodbye.

"Come by the office for a cappuccino sometime," David said. "Or call me if you want to go out on the town. I already know some nice people and locations."

Why not? New friends opened up new perspectives.

6

The first week went by in no time. As in Munich, she started the day with a morning routine. Either she went to the gym around the corner or stirred up her energy with a yoga session at home, followed by a proper portion of fresh fruit with cereal. After reading or listening to the news she went out exploring. There was so much to discover. Each district had its own character, its own charm. Toronto's different places seemed like pieces of a puzzle that had been put together over time.

Christiana had not yet decided which part was her favorite. At times, she was drawn to the Victorian flair of the Distillery District, especially when a jazz concert could be combined with Japanese noodles and cocktails afterwards. Then again she was equally drawn to one of the many small art galleries in the western part of Queen St West. There, she would stroll through the quarter, discover new murals or watch the mélange of people passing by as she sipped on an aperitif in a cozy and undiscovered cafe. Other days, she longed for the hustle and bustle of downtown.

Today, her morning read had put her in a reflective mood. One article had described the potential for injustice that the use of new technologies such as artificial intelligence still brought with them. A French company had developed a facial recognition system, which had already been used by the FBI, but also by the police in France and Australia to identify criminals.

Two new variants had been developed for border controls. However, the test showed that when comparing the faces of black women with photos from a database, the algorithm returned false matches ten times more often than with those of white women. The fewest mistakes were made for men of white skin color. Allegedly, it was due to physical differences, especially in the pigmentation of the skin, which the algorithms processed differently and thus learned at a different pace.

But the systems were developed by humans, meaning the skills and mindset of the development team determined how accurate the systems were. The variety of data used to train them was just as important. And data on darker skin colors was in short supply. Even algorithms developed by industry giants showed errors in people with black skin significantly more often.

What could be done to make people more aware of such differences and ensure they were taken into account when developing new applications? Out of sight, out of mind, the saying went. And not for nothing: if various facets were not present in one's immediate surroundings, they were simply not taken into account. But how was it possible to make people aware of this without immediately being considered an obtrusive do-gooder?

Now she was sitting in the restaurant she had noticed on her very first day. Since then she had become somewhat of a regular. The concept was both simple and full of fantasy. The store had immediately won her heart when she ordered a Poké Bowl with raw fish and vegetables, mango, sushi rice, and spicy sauce at the counter. The cashier had asked her name and then shouted to her kitchen team: "Christiana is doing AMAZING today". Who wouldn't be in a good mood after that?

All dishes had an adjective as a name and were freshly prepared for each order. Another time, when she took her muesli in a recyclable cardboard bowl with compostable cutlery, she was "dreamy". Today, after much deliberation she had decided that she was "grateful". That was true.

Until now, there had only been one situation in which she felt uncomfortable. A man, outwardly just like the many other passers-by in the financial district, had approached her with an unexpected aggressiveness. In the end he hadn't talked to her at all, just seemed to be looking for an outlet to rid himself of his deep-seated despair. Not just a brief outburst of frustration over a failed business deal or an unfortunate meeting, it was a tirade against everything and everyone. But he didn't really seem confused. What tragic thing had happened to this man?

Juggling roasted chickpeas with edamame, fresh zucchini and watermelon radish between the noodles, she thought about what she wanted to do. Exploring the city was fun, but she also wanted something more concrete. But what?

Anything she could help with. She decided to go to Queens Park. Universities always had something inspiring. She zigzagged northwards along the smaller roads away from the major traffic arteries. At the City Hall the oversized lettering with its bright colors stood up against the cloudy sky. But the weather had never had much influence on her mood.

Still shy of Queens Park, she was about to turn left onto College Street when she saw a poster near the Firemen's Monument. Inspired by the sight she turned right without further hesitation. As spontaneous as David was, she was sure he'd love a visit.

"What's cooking?" he greeted her irreverently at reception. "Hopefully not your circuit board," came her prompt reply. "The only thing that's steaming today is my keyboard. I'm coding and in the middle of a tricky challenge. So, thank you for rescuing me before I set my fingers on fire."

The incubator he worked in was located on the sixth floor. From his desk David could see the whole square in front of the building. With the big colorful billboards, it looked a bit like Times Square.

While David showed her around, he exchanged a few friendly words with everybody, whether it was answering a technical question, praising the work of a colleague, letting his fingers fly over the keyboard as he checked a few lines of code, or arranging a meeting over coffee.

For a moment a feeling of loneliness came over her. She was about to say goodbye when David introduced her to a young woman. Ashley was responsible for marketing at the incubator and was an ardent advocate of diversity. The program for black people, in which David participated, was very close to her heart.

Among the Canadian founding partners of the initiative were a major investment bank and a world-leading software company for e-commerce solutions. The program in the incubator was challenging, no question. But it gave the teams the opportunity to work closely with experienced industry experts and mentors from the digital world. They had access to investors and researchers through the university's network. The teams not only had a place to work in the middle of downtown Toronto, but were also supported in their search for affordable housing.

A quarter of an hour and a cappuccino later Christiana had found herself something to do. For some time, Ashley had been looking for someone to help her market the program internationally. Only if enough black people knew about the program and applied would they reach their goal of achieving more diversity in the start-up environment.

It wasn't a full-time job. Christiana was free to organize her time. Someone from the incubator would take care of her work permit. This could happen surprisingly quickly: she would be able to participate in the big technology conference in a few days and support the booth team. Many incubator startups presented their work there in search of customers and new investors.

"This calls for a celebration. What do you say we sail under a black flag tonight?" David said with a conspiratorial wink. "All chillaxed on cool R&B sound.“ At her questioning glance he let her in on the plan.

She was skeptical at first. Normally large water areas were not her thing. For her, the sea was sinister at night. The sound of the waves in the darkness was scary, representing an uncontrollable power. But she didn't want to be a spoilsport. David looked at her with such enthusiasm. She was so pleased that he wanted her to be there. He cocked his head to one side. "Come on, it will be fun. I'll take care of you." How could she refuse? It did sound like an unusual evening. Just how unusual, she would find out soon enough.

7

The thought of her new role had carried her on a comfy cloud the whole afternoon. It was always amazing how fast things could develop. As if some wishes came true by themselves.

The job was perfect. She would meet new people, do something meaningful, and have plenty of time for other things. In the evening she walked all the way across town – still full of energy. Somehow, she felt like Ed Sheeran today. She set the playlist to repeat. In one of his songs it said „overcome your fear". She was really curious what the evening had in store for her.

On the way she noticed a small café across the street. It was unobtrusive, yet had something attractive about it. Maybe it was the name that reminded her of an aunt. On the long wooden counter, homemade biscuits under glass lids lured the guests. One slate listed dishes made from natural and local ingredients. Another with a list of gin cocktails almost tempted her.

Over an espresso, she learned from the barista that the name of the café was a tribute to a street that had long since ceased to exist – at that time it had been very close to the Flat Iron Building, which was officially called the Gooderham Building. The street had been something like the red-light district of the city and had, in the nineteenth century, given a home to people for whom there was no place in society. Then a wave of cholera rolled over the city. Whose fault was it? Naturally enough, those to whom the rich and powerful had sneaked for their lovers' trysts in the shadow of the night.

Christiana arrived at the pier at Lakeshore Boulevard on time. The sky had continued to close in, but it was not raining. David was already standing in front of the ship with a group of young people.

"Here comes our rescue," he shouted, beaming. "Christiana will rock us over the waves with her sensitive voice today," he turned to his friends. She was so baffled that she started to laugh out loud.

"What on earth gave you that idea?" she asked, still chuckling. "You already have fans here you didn't know about," he winked. It soon transpired that his neighbor had heard Christiana in her apartment in the morning. "I'm sure you're not singing just for fun," Verena said appreciatively.

The singer of the band due to play at the boat trip had fallen ill at short notice. When looking at the planned set list, Christiana noticed only one song that she didn't know. She really felt like singing. Now was not the time to think about the impact her decision might have. Nothing else stood in the way of an unforgettable evening.

Before she went on board, she felt a little queasy as the twilight bathed everything in a dim light. The pirate flag and the wooden boat, smaller than she had imagined, gave the whole thing an air of adventure. They left the safe harbor. From the railing the water seemed much closer than she would have liked. There were almost no seats on the boat, the waves putting her sense of balance to the test.

The softly whispered conversations, short video recordings, and applause after each song gave her encouragement. Soon it felt like a family reunion and she forgot about her fear of the sea. During a break she was talking to a man who was about her age.

Hamoun had largely grown up in Toronto and had not

travelled much in his youth. He was making up for it now. Travel had become a passion. It showed him other cultures and ways of thinking. South Africa and Asia were among his favorites. Singapore was okay, but he liked Seoul better. A few years ago, influenced by the enthusiastic stories of friends, he had gone to Taiwan, where he had now founded his second company.

Environmental protection and sustainable living were important to him. That was why he had developed a sensor to measure the fill level of garbage cans and transmit this information by radio. Far too often garbage bins were emptied too early. This was not only unnecessary but also increased traffic and air pollution. His solution offered a high savings potential, which ultimately benefited the environment again. For the next two weeks he visited his sister, who was also on the boat and still lived in Toronto. It had become windier and started drizzling. She sneezed. Hamoun immediately brought her a blanket. Most of the others had also wrapped themselves up.

The view of the city was nevertheless beautiful and relatively clear. After five more songs they moored at the pier again. In retrospect, the trip felt much shorter than two hours, but the evening was far from over.

David had reserved a table for everyone in a hip fish restaurant. Christiana was curious whether the oysters were catered to the cocktails or vice versa. As it turned out, there was also lobster and various types of finger food. Verena, their neighbor, was balancing a plate and a glass of white in her left hand while nibbling off a skewer. Her freckles and red hair glowed under the ceiling lamp.

She had been in the city for some time. She worked as a freelance photographer and copywriter and created video portraits. Her lifeblood hung on stories – whether read, filmed, cut, shaken or stirred. She loved meeting new people, hearing about their unusual experiences and then putting them in the right setting. Smiling, she showed Christiana some pictures taken on the boat. The clique stood opposite her and seemed fixated by her performance. It was almost as if they were dancing.

Verena had needed a moment to realize that she had to pay special attention to lighting conditions. Otherwise the singer would melt into the night sky. Christiana laughed out loud. "I've heard that before. Very few people think about it at first because they're not used to it." Her skin color had another side effect. If she was not well – no matter if she was carrying a flu or a hangover – it was not immediately obvious. She didn't turn pale because of it, she winked.

Looking at the photos Christiana was very pleased with how she looked. Between bites she learned that Verena's great dream was to enrich the world and make it more colorful – with the stories and visions of people whose voice deserved to be heard. Christiana got goose bumps.

How, in such a short time, was it possible to encounter people with whom she had so much in common?

8

Her work permit arrived just in time for the big technology conference. Christiana met with Ashley to discuss the details. During the three days she would help out at the stand for a few hours in the morning. The rest of the time she was free to listen to talks or stroll around. Ashley gave her plenty of material about the incubator and the four-month scholarship for black people who wanted to push their founding idea.

Summer weather was forecasted for the weekend and Christiana decided that a day at the lake was just the right thing for reading through the documents. The only question was whether she wanted to go to one of the islands or to the beach in the east of the city tomorrow. David had texted her. He was meeting a few people at the brewery on the old railway premises in the evening. Beer wasn't really her thing, but a fun evening was. And, with their little gang, the evenings were always fun.

Everyone was sitting at the bar when she came in. Verena and Hamoun were hatching some idea. David had put his arm around a young woman whose countless blonde curls danced the tango with his braids. Both seemed to be happily stranded on their own island in the middle of the hustle and bustle. Christiana hugged Verena and Hamoun as a greeting and ordered a Munich Lager. Something that reminded her of home.

Next to her sat a woman who was talking to the manager. Both, she noticed, liked riding motorcycle. As luck would have it, they relieved her of the decision of which beach to go to tomorrow. Apparently, parts of the islands in Lake Ontario were still flooded by the melted snow. It would be The Beaches, east of the city, then.

Hamoun nudged her and let her and Verena, mischievously, in on how he had landed in a hush bar the other day after the pirate ship trip. Her questioning look encouraged him to continue. He had moved on from the fish restaurant with some of the boys to a club. After a few drinks they had discovered that there was a hidden side door leading to a small secret bar. It was almost like being in a spy film.

People whose acquaintance most other people only made through the cover of glossy business magazines sat and stood there with drinks in hand. Hamoun had taken heart and pitched his start-up to a well-known, billionaire investor. He seemed to be more than only politely interested.

"You really give it your all," Christiana laughed appreciatively as she ordered her second beer. It was, against all expectations, very drinkable. Suddenly David noticed her. "Hey Chrissy – cool to see you. Leni here is my other half," he introduced his girlfriend with a warm look.

Leni had a smile that brought back the most beautiful childhood memories. She still lived in Berlin, but the two could never be separated for very long. She was a passionate photographer and worked for various companies as a brand ambassador. Christiana liked her style right away. She wore a wide cut white suit, which gave her a casual yet feminine elegance that was playful at the same time. Leni would come to Toronto more often in the near future.

Maybe she would even move here. Because she liked the city. But she also loved Berlin.

9

The next morning Christiana drove the faint feeling of fatigue away with a walk out to the distillery. From there she went up to Queen St to take the tram to the beach. It was a lovely day. The sun shone warmly and a light wind moved refreshingly through the streets.

The tram ride took her past low brick houses, which changed from offices to residential buildings. The neighborhood after the bridge over the Don River did not seem particularly attractive to her. A few blocks further to the west it became more cheerful again. Colorful buildings with cafés and restaurants, on whose outdoor terraces families with children enjoyed their weekend breakfast, alternated with small shops. The closer she came to "The Beaches", the tidier and more homelike the area seemed to her.

She got off at Kew Gardens and walked down a side street lined with tall trees. The closer she came to the lake shore, the more comfortable the houses looked. Flowers adorned verandas, hammocks on balconies invited the residents to read or sleep, and in almost every well-kept garden there was a barbecue. On the wooden beach promenade, open-air life was already in full swing.

She mingled with people who pushed baby carriages, walked dogs on a leash, linked arms with each other or jogged past her alone at breakneck speed. Families picnicked on the relatively wide sandy beach while toddlers were busy building castles. Lovers sunbathed, bodies entangled. Occasionally she saw a brave swimmer who had defied the cool temperature of the lake and was apparently receiving recognition from the seagulls.

A display board proudly explained the meaning of the blue flag fluttering in the wind: it was the international award for high water quality and cleanliness and safety on the beach, and also for environmentally friendly actions and management.

After about half an hour she arrived at a beach club with a raised terrace just before the end of the promenade. A good time to have a cappuccino in the sun. All tables were occupied. Coffee in hand she went back to the promenade, where one of the cheerful-looking wooden chairs, which could be seen all over the city, had just become free.

To her right sat a woman whose light strands of hair shone in the sun like liquid gold through her dark, almost shoulder-length curls. She looked up from her book and greeted Christiana with a warm smile. Marie, as she soon introduced herself, was allowing herself a short break outside before picking up her son Adam from hockey training and preparing a big dinner with her family.

When Christiana told her that she came from Bavaria and that one of her favorites parts of Toronto was the Distillery district, Marie was thrilled. She had grown up in Lebanon. After graduating from high school, she moved to the USA to study marketing and international business. What she particularly liked about Kansas State University was its internationality: most of her friends came from France or Germany. Besides Europeans, the university was also home to many students from Africa, Asia or Latin America.

Christiana gave a laugh when Marie mentioned how everyone at work had called her the Computer Lab Girl as apart from her there were only four male assistants. In the end, her IT system career had lasted only one Visual Basic course. Programming wasn't her thing. Marie enjoyed working with computers, but not when it came to searching for a missing dot in millions of lines of code.

"I admire people who have the patience for that," she said. Christiana nodded in agreement and thought of the fun David had with it. Marketing and eCommerce were all the more important to Marie. After her studies she had started as an analyst in the field and completed her MBA on the side. Then, seven years ago, she had emigrated here.

At that time, there were few people in Canada who specialized in the use of digital technologies, particularly in eCommerce. At first she was discouraged owing to the lack of job opportunities. Ultimately, however, in combination with her French language skills, this proved to be her trump card.

Her experience in the field had enabled her to assist in the development of digital strategies for user experience and customer satisfaction. Now she worked for one of the world's largest development aid organizations, whose Canadian office in Mississauga was located just east of Toronto.

In all her work with the church at home, Christiana had not yet given much thought to how humanitarian aid had to keep up with digitalization. It seemed logical and sensible to apply the same principles to donations as to the marketing of consumer goods. „How exactly do you do that?" she asked Marie.

"In principle, it is important that people who want to donate feel that visiting the website is as pleasant as possible in all areas, that they are well informed and that they donate directly to our projects."

The office therefore collected data on how visitors used

the website and how often this resulted in donations. The data was evaluated and factual conclusions were drawn. These in turn were passed on within the organization to the team of colleagues with suggestions for priorities, who then adapted the website and optimized campaigns. The evaluated data could then help everyone in the team with their e-mails, newsletters or meetings. After all, as in normal companies, the aim was to maximize the ROI: the more donations that could be raised with as little internal effort as possible, the better for the projects benefitting from the development aid.

What Marie liked most about her work was that she could learn something new every day and share it with others from different teams. She was particularly attracted by new challenges. She had always loved puzzles where she could critically examine things and take different perspectives. The answers and solutions to them were the greatest reward. "Enough about me," Marie waved. "What brings you to Toronto?"

Christiana pondered for a moment and laughed. "I'm looking for answers, too, only my puzzle is a little more complex." She talked about the voice inside her and the feeling that a new job was waiting for her.

Marie nodded impressively. "It's super brave of you to just go to a strange place for half a year without knowing what to expect. I don't know if I could do that." Though Marie was more concerned with security, she shared a belief with Christiana: it was important to trust in one's own decisions. Even if some things did not develop as desired, later the events often made sense. Letting go and trusting that the pieces of the puzzle would fit together made many things easier. But letting go was not always easy.

She would have loved to stay and talk more. After a

glance at her watch, Marie had to say goodbye. She quickly wrote her phone number on a piece of paper. Maybe one day they would visit Niagara Falls or go hiking together?

Christiana remained in the sun and pulled the incubator documents from her bag. After she had read everything carefully three times, she strolled back towards the city along the shore. It was already late afternoon, but the day was too beautiful for tram rides. She decided to walk most of the way. Strolling past the beach volleyball courts, she thought back to the conversation with Marie. It was fascinating.

How was it that the universe kept providing encounters like this seemingly at random?

10

The conference started late Monday afternoon, but she had already picked up her ticket in the morning to avoid long queues. After all, almost 25,000 visitors were expected at the Enercare Center.

Not surprising given the list of speakers, which included far more stars than asterisks: first and foremost, Canada's Prime Minister and Toronto's Mayor, followed by globally successful founders and leaders of the international tech scene, government representatives and big names from show business. Thanks to their participation, the technology conference was considered the fastest growing in North America.

Christiana had a little time before it started. She decided

to go for a walk by the lake. She did not have an umbrella with her, but she took the risk. Who knew how much fresh air she would get in the next few days? Her list included more talks than she could attend, not to mention the exhibiting companies, organizations and start-ups that interested her.

She went down Lakeshore Boulevard to the lakeside promenade. The now familiar wooden chairs defied the uncomfortable gusts with their gay colors. Sun rays fought with the clouds. It was a standoff. Sailboats sloshed on the wind-driven waves in the small harbor on the shore. A plane took to the sky, soon leaving the short runway of Hanlan's Point on Toronto Island behind it. How many business people would be landing at this small airport because of the conference?

Apparently it was used a lot, especially for domestic flights. That would explain why there was even an underwater tunnel next to the ferry. Pedestrians were able to access the terminal on roller conveyors. Christiana had just fended off a swarm of tiny flies when she registered a small, rapidly growing point in the distance.

An unmistakable, cheeky rocking of the head betrayed him from afar. David sprinted towards her. „Hey, sunshine. Gone with the wind?" he shouted happily to her. „Almost. What are you running on today?" she replied, laughing.

The words tumbled out of him at world-record speed. He had a new idea, a new concept. It was different from the original one, but somehow still connected to it. "Let me tell you in peace. Breakfast tomorrow?" He ran again. "I'm at the conference till Thursday," she shouted after him. "I'll call you." He turned halfway around with a thumbs-up gesture, ran on and soon disappeared behind the trees.

What a livewire, she smiled. Always good for a surprise. Christiana walked to the small marina opposite the IMAX cinema and enjoyed the city skyline. A gull was sailing above her in the wind. A short gust pushed it to the right, but that did not disturb the bird. With a short wing beat it adapted to the new conditions. There was so much one could learn from nature. Christiana was looking forward to everything that her time here had in store for her.

And now it was time for the conference. She didn't want to miss the Prime Minister's opening speech.

11

Christiana meandered past the long rows of visitors who still had to get their ticket. She got a seat in one of the first rows in front of the main stage. Opportunity favored the prepared mind. The light was dimmed. The air seemed to crackle. Audience expectations were enhanced by the stage set.

It was a mixture of iron throne and fire reminiscent of a successful TV series. The music supported the theme. Many of the series' fans came from the tech environment. When the founder of the conference stepped onto the stage, applause broke out. Loud, approving whistles greeted him. Paddy was responsible for three tech conferences in total, he and his team achieving worldwide success in less than a decade.

The European conference in Lisbon was the largest ever with 70,000 visitors. That demanded respect. The North American version had its roots in Las Vegas and, after a few years in New Orleans, had now landed in Toronto. Here it would stay for at least the next three years.

The organizer was particularly proud of the many countries – 120 in all – from which the participants came today. Networking was the most important part of the conference for him, so he asked everyone to stand up briefly and introduce themselves to their neighbors. Because you never knew who was sitting next to you or behind you. Christiana loved surprises like this. And she was not disappointed either.

When she turned around, a man with a dark blond full beard smiled at her. He introduced himself as Justin, an Executive Director of the Media Lab in the Big Apple. The lab was born out of a partnership between the media industry of New York and its universities. Bertelsmann, Bloomberg, Hearst, Audible, Shutterstock and the New York Times were just some of the prominent partners. Through the lab, they had contact with students researching various technologies at the city's universities. There they could also build prototypes for new applications directly with them. As well as this the lab connected the partners with various start-ups and offered intrapreneurship programs via the Venture Platform and the Combine Accelerator.

Christiana could well imagine that this approach was successful. The media industry in particular had been faced with many challenges due to increasing digitalization. In his second role as recent founder Justin had created the first city-funded center for virtual and augmented reality in the Brooklyn Navy Yard, covering 1,500 square meters. Here new spaces and future technologies were explored. Prototypes were built, and partnerships between newly founded companies and corporations that wanted to boost their innovation were made possible.

On the stage Paddy asked for silence again. There

hadn't been enough time. Christiana had the feeling that Justin would have liked to talk longer as well. He gave her a card. Would they continue their conversation in the next few days?

To great applause, the Prime Minister of Canada entered the stage for his interview with the founder of a digital media company that was, in worldwide online video, snapping at the heels of the Mountain View Internet giant.

Christiana had never heard of Shahrzad or her company and immediately searched the internet for information: she was born in Iran and emigrated to Canada in her teens. The company had been founded about 15 years ago, shortly after Shahrzad had completed her degree in computer studies, and had been grown through partnerships with big names like NBA, Sony Pictures and Viacom.

Its success was based on using not only financial metrics, but also considering the impact on employees, the community, and the environment. Many prestigious awards recognized her approach. She had more in common with Justin Trudeau than just this interview.

In 2018, he selected her as the Canadian representative for the Business Women Leaders Working Group to work with representatives of participating governments at the G20 Summit in Buenos Aires, Argentina, and develop workable solutions for empowering women in business. Diversity was therefore a major theme on stage, since one of the most important issues for the tech industry was access to good personnel. How could this be guaranteed?

According to the Prime Minister, immigration policy played the most important role, alongside education at home. While other large countries tended to close up their borders, Canada pursued the opposite goal. The so-called „Global Skills Strategy" enabled top people from all over the world to gain a foothold in the country within two weeks.

The Prime Minister firmly believed that the 350,000 or so immigrants who arrived every year had a positive effect: they helped to make neighborhoods stronger, more resilient and thus more livable. At the same time, the government was aware that local residents needed to be offered a way to see a future for themselves. Where digitization was concerned, it was especially important to invest in education and research programs. This included programming courses in primary and secondary schools.

The clear message was that in Canada everyone could be successful. At present, unemployment was at a 40-year low. Innovation often took place in large cities like Vancouver or Toronto. At the same time, however, apartment and house prices had risen sharply, and transport connections were variable. Mobility and affordable housing were essential, the media founder said.

That's why there were special programs for this, the head of government explained. On the one hand, 180 billion dollars were invested in infrastructure projects, such as the expansion of the public rail system and local transport. On the other hand, there were buying incentives for young people to buy houses without fees and mortgage interest. Smart City competitions were intended to promote innovative ideas.

Christiana thought of a project in Toronto, which one of her colleagues was following with great enthusiasm. The problem was that the lab responsible belonged to the same holding company as the world's largest internet data kraken. Was the benefit of the general public really that project's principal?

As if the Prime Minister had read her mind, he began explaining another important goal – he wanted to stop

Canadian start-ups from making their companies big just to sell them to the IT giants for a lot of money. Silicon Valley was not the only breeding ground for successful companies. On the contrary.

Here in Canada the standard of living was higher and there were more available, well-trained personnel. Funding programs had been set up to support young founders. Artificial intelligence had been declared a focus topic. 125 million dollars were available for investment.

When asked by Shahrzad about his „elevator pitch" for Canada, Justin Trudeau did not have to think long: stability and diversity, coupled with access to two-thirds of the world's available gross domestic product. For Canada was the only country in the G7 community that had free trade agreements with all the others.

Foreign companies wishing to take advantage of this with a branch office found a contact point in the „Invest in Canada" initiative, which offered them everything they needed from one source. In addition to all the positive information on diversity, there was one topic that the moderator had kept to herself until the end: the gender pay gap. Her company paid women and men in equal positions the same amount.

The Prime Minister admitted that there was still some catching up to be done in this area and appealed to the companies present. He was convinced that more positions at all levels, including top management, should be filled by women. This was not only morally right; it was the right thing to do. The interview ended with enthusiastic applause, which only subsided when the official opening of the conference was announced on stage.

Christiana was also impressed. But was Canada really the land of opportunity? It was difficult to judge how positive things were in reality. One thing in particular would interest her.

To what extent had women or female founders working in the artificial intelligence branch been supported by the state?

12

The next morning, she was assigned to booth duty. Christiana literally jumped out of bed. She wanted to be on time anyway in case of a possible delay at the entrance.

The sun had won its bet against the clouds this morning. The trees in the park below her apartment stood as still as statues. The wind had died down, even though it was still fresh. A good opportunity to walk to the Exhibition Place.

She took Bathurst Street. Just before the railway bridge there was a small area on the right, where containers were stacked and packed against each other. A quick glance revealed that each of them housed a small shop or office. Further back there was a Belgian brewery. She continued on to the green hill of Fort York.

There a path led below the Gardiner Expressway. While weeds normally reigned in chaos beneath highway bridges, they were completely absent here. The Bentway was a new, public space created at the beginning of 2018. She had read somewhere that the site was created thanks to the generous 25 million dollar donation of a respected Toronto city planner.

Hardly anyone else was out and about on the clean and tidy pavements made of concrete slabs or wooden panels. She walked past some small works of art and stopped briefly at two open containers with exhibition objects. The area offered a lot of space for a wide variety of events. Maybe she should go to one of the regular Tai Chi and Yoga sessions?

She had also read that people from the neighborhood met here on some evenings during the summer to eat together. Each dinner had a different motto: there were Indian, Caribbean, Filipino, Spanish, Syrian or even Tibetan specialties. Everything was prepared directly on site by selected guest chefs. On Sundays, local musicians took the opportunity to win new fans among the local residents.

Christiana made a mental note. David and the gang would go for this for sure. There were also presentations, training sessions and art demonstrations, including hands-on workshops on growing vegetables in the city with minimal water use. In winter the paths became an ice rink where the whole family could indulge in frosty fun. At that thought, Christiana was suddenly not so cold anymore.

She hurried towards the building, wondering what surprises the day had in store for her.

13

The atmosphere in the huge hall was a mix of hectic preparations and ecstatic anticipation. Startup founders tapped through their pitch decks on PCs or polished exhibits until glossy. Others, alternating with colleagues, simulated interviews with investors, at pains to think of every conceivable question. Company representatives set up tables for discussions with potential customers.

In a large, greenhouse-like pavilion, pillows and headphones were ready for meditation seekers. In between, she saw a number of ceiling-high, black, sound-absorbing fabric walls. Behind the pavilion, stages were ready for the industry's big players. Each stage was dedicated to a different theme with a correspondingly hip design.

Christiana savored the hustle and bustle around her. When she arrived at the booth, her colleagues showed her where to find everything, especially the important things: good cappuccino and the nearest toilet. It was so exciting to be in the middle of all this. The morning passed in fast motion.

Only one situation caused confusion at first and then irritation. The fire alarm. Just a technical problem, the announcers stated calmly. When the siren, which sounded at half-minute intervals, finally stopped after twenty minutes, everyone breathed a sigh of relief and normality resumed.

With each conversation Christiana found it easier to explain the program for black founders to the conference's open-minded visitors. Many took a brochure with them.

Some had a friend or acquaintance the program might be suitable for. Others worked for companies that could imagine supporting the project financially. Programs designed to promote diversity were on the rise.

Early adopters, as risk-taking early supporters were called, really saw a mutual benefit in this. It was only a matter of time before it was in vogue, and the masses jumped on the bandwagon. At least that was the firm belief of Christiana's colleagues at the booth.

From the lunch break onwards she was off. After a quick salad she went to the main stage. The former CEO of the company which had made its fortune with their short messages was being interviewed by the co-founder of an American technology blog.

She had sold her company, which specialized in news about Californian technology companies and held an annual conference on the subject, to a major digital media company a few years ago. She was known in the industry for not mincing her words and addressing things directly.

The first thing she wanted to know, of course, was whether he had left the company because of all the problems caused by the American president. His response was, as expected, rather diplomatic in nature. His incentive in a time when social media had to reinvent itself was to provide users with even more communication and entertainment – especially when it was good and relevant.

To achieve this, he wanted to create an ad-free and independent platform full of ideas, insights, knowledge, opinions and perspectives – from people from all over the world for people from all over the world. He considered his current company to be a place that brought together independent and curious people online and combined professional journalism with contributions from readers. The platform was best suited for texts that were too short for a blog post but too long for a tweet.

He also wanted to invest wisely, especially in companies that were committed to sustainability, health, diversity and social justice; that offered positive solutions to the world's problems and did not belong to the typical Silicon Valley bro cults. Christiana could only agree with him. In her opinion, the last two points in particular were more important than ever.

The next contribution on another stage went in a similar direction. Christiana's new acquaintance from New York talked to a reporter from one of the most popular media portals in the English-speaking world. Their mixture of blog, news ticker and online magazine was only partly created by their own journalists; the main part was generated by the users.

The two discussed the relationship between social media and traditional publishers and whether both could coexist. According to Justin, the two areas were in a kind of separation phase. Large news companies did use social media platforms to distribute their articles. But their main focus was to lure readers to their own pages.

In social media, independent reporting was mixed with contributions from so-called influencers: people who had a lot of time and many followers, but who were usually only after personal gain. Publishers, on the other hand, had to finance their editorial offices through advertisements on their sites. Especially small, local news outlets found this difficult. That's why there were fewer and fewer of them.

The sophisticated algorithms of Google, Facebook and co. preferred large advertising budgets which small companies did not have. One solution could be to tax the revenues of major advertising platforms. The money could go into a fund that financed democratically reliable news and fact-finding, down to the local level.

This raised another important question. Were there enough young people these days who wanted to learn the profession of journalism? Journalism degrees were still popular among students, Justin said. So far, so good. However, many young people found Silicon Valley giants attractive as potential employers. The latter should therefore be held more accountable, or even dismembered, especially with regard to the use of new technologies such as 5G, artificial intelligence or neural networks.

Christiana was reminded of a conversation she had had with David. He had explained that neural networks were just a subset of the artificial intelligence field and regarding them as a separate category was redundant. Still, it was probably only data scientists or people working in the machine-learning field who were aware of this distinction. David also wouldn't call AI a new technology, though he did acknowledge that neural nets were being used in a novel way.

Today their use was mostly facilitated by the rapid development of GPUs over the past two decades which significantly brought down the cost of compute resources. That was the reason why 5G and AI would shake up whole industries. On stage, Justin was sure the news landscape would be no exception. International developments could also not be ignored.

Who knew where the next influential platform would be? Asia, especially China, was catching up fast.

14

At the thought of China, an icy shiver ran down Christiana's spine. Technology there seemed to be the tool for a totalitarian surveillance regime. Officially, it was always about ensuring the safety of the people in the country. Social networks and networked devices played a decisive role. It was therefore not surprising that large corporations from China were seeking contracts with other cities around the world to make them „smart". The collected data flowed into the home country, were evaluated there and expanded the Chinese government's insight abroad.

In pilot projects in various Chinese cities, locals had already been evaluated according to a „social" points system. Reward the good, punish the bad. It was that simple. Conclusions about their credibility were drawn from their actions. It was not yet clear how comprehensive the evaluation was. The technical possibilities opened the door to conspiracy theorists.

After all, the highest court in the country already had blacklists. It listed persons who had been sentenced to fines and not yet paid them. Or insulted someone and not yet apologized. A place on the list meant: no place on the express train or plane; no access for the children to private schools.

The youngest inhabitants were already monitored in detail. Robots in preschools checked the little ones for their health. In schools, children had to wear electronic headbands that measured their brain waves. Students at universities were monitored even more closely. Access by facial recognition only. Attention control by cameras in classrooms. That was so blatant, Christiana thought.

A smiling face tore her from her thoughts. "Hey, good to see you," Marie embraced her with joy. "You look worried," she added. Drawing on the information she had just heard Christiana expressed frustration at how technology was starting to impinge on our freedoms.

Marie could only shake her head in agreement. She was part of Generation X, had grown up with the internet and witnessed the exponential growth firsthand. While still a student the first online chat services had satisfied her hunger. In two ways. Long conversations with her remote family were now so much cheaper, leaving enough money for healthy food. Soon after completing her degree she got rid of her TV, preferring to stream her favorite shows on her PC. Today things were even more comfortable because the TV was online.

The internet had brought about a radical change in the last decade. Old procedures were replaced by new ones. Companies' long-established on the market were displaced by inventive founders with their new business models. A life without the internet seemed almost impossible today. Especially for young people. They were tech-savvy and knew the advantages. Especially when it came to shopping. That's why they expected added value everywhere – whether in the online shop or in the shop around the corner. Advertising on their preferred platforms should only offer things that were to their own taste.

Marie sighed. "I hope, however, that in future it will be even more about quality and credible information that I can trust. It doesn't help much if I'm constantly being shown the same walking poles just because I've looked at them once," she said. Christiana frowned. "But doesn't even more specific information also mean that more data about me needs to be collected and evaluated with artificial intelligence?"

"That's right," nodded Marie. Still, she believed that the internet could soon change fundamentally. More data protection. More information for users on how and for what purposes their data was collected. Perhaps there was even a way to return to an approach similar to the original concept of the internet? So that the sharing of knowledge again played the key role. Inwardly, Christiana wished the same. But was that really possible? After all, more and more people used web browsers that allowed neutral searches and protected their privacy.

Marie always had at least these browsers open in parallel when she was surfing. She found search engines in standard browsers to be extremely limiting. "The only things that learn are the algorithms." Due to her online behavior, her profile has been continuously refined. Everything she saw was tailored to her. There was no room for independent thinking, for vision and diverse views. "It is time to find solutions that will endure in the long run," she said with a fiery look in her eyes.

Solutions that were not about short-term profit. But where did you find people who thought like that?

15

After promising Marie that she would be in contact again soon, Christiana let herself drift through the exhibition. As she strolled past the young startups, a stand seemed to speak to her directly. The founder radiated an energy that immediately aroused curiosity. What was her business?

It was something Christiana was passionate about: eating. Far too much food was carelessly thrown away. The environment and the wallet were the victims. There were already apps available to help with this. Most of them focused on the monetary aspect. That was okay and legitimate. A bakery or restaurant could, as soon as it knew how much food would be left at the end of the day, offer food and meals for half price or less.

Businesses reduced their losses. Customers saved money and still enjoyed good food that would otherwise have landed in the bin. Many of the apps gradually rolled out their service worldwide. But Ivonne thought in a slightly different direction. She wasn't in it to make a quick buck. Her thinking was more local. When her circle of friends met, they would refuse to buy extra supplies. Usually one of their refrigerators was too full, and the other too empty. The same, of course, applied to people's purses.

That was why her concept helped everyone. Many groceries from the shops in their vicinity were thrown away. That was terrible and still happened too often. Of course, locals could choose the more lucrative solutions. But what if the money from the sales was used for a good cause nearby?

It was like donating. Only more directly. Instead of bills, salad, sandwiches or spaghetti changed hands. No matter whether it was from business, company celebrations or other events. Anything was possible as long as the expiration date had not been reached.

Privately, the whole thing worked the same way. Those who had gone shopping with eyes bigger than their stomachs could spare others a hungry night. With a few clicks, a guilty conscience could morph into a feeling of happiness. Maybe someone had just cooked for the extended family, but basket-ball training had finished late, and plans had been changed. Then the children of a single parent, who had been stuck at work all day, could come home to a steaming plate of delicious pasta. So people could pass "meatballs" to each other.

One of the projects provided students in Calgary with thousands of lunches every day. "Share-Eat-Repeat" sounded like a wonderful motto. Christiana was delighted. Also, because Yvonne radiated a warm-heartedness that made her ambition credible. She had given her the link to download the app in Canada. Christiana was about to share it with the gang. Wasn't it true that "sharing was caring"?

As she was typing the message, one came from David. "Hungry?" Sometimes he really scared her. It was as if he could read minds. The conference was almost over for today. Inspired by the meeting with Ivonne, she suggested they meet at someone's home. It didn't matter whose. None of them had to go far. Whatever the kitchen could provide was put on the table. And that, as it turned out, was something to be proud of: pasta with truffles.

16

David seemed even more energetic than usual. He was still buzzing with ideas; one in particular. He enjoyed working in the incubator, no question. But his original approach was not social enough, too commercial.

That only helped the big companies get even bigger. The logistics world was complex, and there was no lack of challenges for autonomous transport systems. The growing number of online orders required more and more resources to deliver the goods. Convenience spread rapidly. People worked long hours in the office, had no time or even the desire to go shopping after work or on weekends. Everyone was looking forward to what free time they had – comfortable on the sofa at home, in restaurants, museums, clubs – whether fitness or fun, in parks or outdoors in nature. That was understandable.

But what about the people who were almost always at home? People who could no longer move freely? Who were denied all the benefits of the outside world because of age, infirmity or illness? That kept him awake at night. He wanted to find a solution to that. The concept for autonomous systems could also be adapted to this target group. Even if it wasn't hip. Young people rarely thought about age. A glance at the most hyped startups proved this. Even when it came to health issues, fitness, rather than simply wellbeing, was often the main focus. David didn't think it was fair.

With Christiana, he was breaking down open doors. But how could his idea be implemented? He hadn't gone to the office today. He went to the museum. He loved those places. They nurtured his inspiration, enabled him to develop new ideas. First, he had gone to the Royal Ontario Museum. It was not far from Toronto University and was one of the largest museums in North America with more than six million exhibits.

One part was of course dedicated to Canada, its biodiversity and the Native Americans. But one could also dive into a multitude of other worlds. Samurais and tea ceremonies in Japan. South Korea and its influence on printing techniques. The lush life of the Egyptians or Romans. Developments from the early Middle East, which were often the foundation of today's technologies. Lost cultures from Africa. Europe and its styles through the ages. Dinosaurs. An area where thousands of species were admired and brought to life through digital animation.

David was particularly fascinated by an exhibition about Africa, America and the Asia-Pacific region, which was dedicated to the diversity of humanity. "The African part reminded me of my youth; and of the gold mine where I worked for a year before I went to college."

Christiana frowned. "This was certainly no easy year." David nodded. But his impressions of the day did not allow for gloomy thoughts.

In the afternoon he had gone to the Ontario Science Center. After voyaging into space and entering a rainforest that had come to life, he had experimented with the limitations of the human body. What was going on in a person who dived without an oxygen tank or climbed Mount Everest? He also showed Christiana a photo of what he would look like in old age.

He had tried out how theories in research were distorted

by prevailing assumptions. After all, race, gender or origin played an enormous role, but were only considered to a limited extent. Unilateral views frowned upon alternative approaches. Fascinated and at the same time frightened by the results, he quickly moved on.

In the end, he had been captivated by a 464-year-old tree. Markers detailed the historical events which had happened in that time. The mere proximity to this natural wonder imbued him with admiration and respect, an almost loving feeling that flowed through him up to his fingertips. As if the aura of the tree was touching his own. She sensed what David meant. He was so much more energetic than usual, which she had almost never thought possible.

"Nature has such an indescribable influence on us," he said. "After the research section, I felt crushed. Two minutes later I'm sitting in front of a tree and I feel like I could literally pull it out." It was precisely this energy that had encouraged him to rethink his project. Set a different focus.

Instead of goods he wanted to move people. So that those who were physically or otherwise limited were not crushed by loneliness within their own four walls. So they could be mobile. Out in nature: getting new energy. Now he only had to convince the team in the incubator.

And if they didn't go along with him? Then Christiana was convinced he'd find another way.

17

The next morning, she was back at the stand an hour before the official opening. She enjoyed the relative peace and quiet during a second cappuccino to get in the mood for the day ahead. The morning was over even faster than the day before. This was not only due to the visitors who came to them.

Christiana felt much safer. She addressed passers-by who caught her eye and could possibly be candidates for the program directly. She had a good nose for them. Her colleagues were quite taken with her and were reluctant to let her go in the early afternoon. But that was the deal. There were some things in the program that interested her.

The first discussion was moderated by a journalist who dealt with the human side of the technology environment. The theme on stage immediately reminded Christiana of David. It was about desire and devotion. Two things that two black stars, an NFL star and an R&B singer, thought were essential on the road to success. But that alone was not enough. Overcoming fears and finding the right partners was just as important. People who shared the same values. The door was open to anyone who was in the right place at the right time. Even more important was to believe in yourself and your own abilities. Sometimes support came out of the blue.

A cellmate had encouraged the musician, who was briefly stranded in prison, to follow his passion for music. To dare and reach for the stars. Later, a second, key experience turned the by then successful singer into an entrepreneur. During one of his concerts in Africa the power went out. A stroke of luck for the people of that continent, as it turned out. Because now the R&B singer set himself the goal of guaranteeing a secure power supply. Thanks to him, more than 600 million people in Africa had by now been supplied with solar energy – despite numerous teething difficulties.

The football star knew exactly what startup difficulties were and how they could be overcome. He had been nominated for the Super Bowl. Then, just a few weeks before the game, he had broken his leg. That was the end of his career, they said. No one could get back on their feet that quickly, let alone play the game. But he believed in his own abilities. He was convinced that he could do it. After seven weeks, he stood tall on the playing field. Even his experienced doctors, who expected many months of convalescence, had underestimated the power of his own convictions.

The next talk was about believing in one's own ability as well. The head of animation production at a major American film studio gave insights behind the scenes of the comic world. More than 800 creative people from various fields of computer-aided animation worked on the new film production about the spidery comic hero.

It was all about giving the audience a new, incredible and unprecedented experience. An animated film that brought the comic to life, breaking all boundaries and opening up new worlds for visual storytelling. In the style of a comic book, the new film included fast and abrupt color transitions, dramatic camera angles, a touch of imperfection, and the hero who had been popular for years, yet was completely new. The result of numerous visualization experiments and a unique combination of 3D animation and 2D visualization was a comic book that came to life – and had won an Academy Award.

Animation also played a significant role in everyday life, Christiana heard the founder and CEO of the American online database for GIFs say on stage. He compared his search engine with the giant from Mountain View. There, the main task was to find facts. However, their research had shown that only about one percent of the entire human vocabulary was used during searches.

Words expressing feelings such as love, joy or hunger were rarely included. They were more important in personal relationships. Therefore, his focus was on interpersonal communication. He had created the platform knowing that moving images could say more within a second than words or explanations.

After six years, people searched for colorful animations around one billion times a day and the number was growing steadily. Some of the searches were pretty crazy. More and more people reacted with gestures and stories or emotions and impressions packed into a GIF when they talked to others online. Seven billion had been sent so far. This development was not surprising. With increasing time pressure and information overload, the moving images seemed to have touched a nerve among users.

Christiana also used the service. It made it easy to send an answer or request to someone during a break or between two meetings without much effort. Short, crisp and funny. Her hearty laughter after some of these messages had often cheered up the office. That's why the platform was not only interesting in the private sector. Customers who felt they were being taken seriously counted among the most loyal. This also applied to millennials. Christiana often had the feeling that she and her friends were a particular target of companies.

18

Millennials were also an extremely interesting target group in another respect, as she discovered at the next talk, especially when it came to games. According to the studio boss at one of the world's leading game providers, the world of „gamers" was constantly growing. She, the studio boss, was an avowed optimist and loved to play. No wonder she liked how the gaming world was developing. But not only from a commercial perspective.

Among the people who often liked to play were millennials and Generation Z. Television debates on climate change, political differences and data protection problems could not throw them off their stride. Still, this wasn't about sitting passively in front of a screen, but interacting daily with people from all over the world. In games, players learned to think strategically and to question facts, but also to work in a team and to support each other. Problems could be best solved together. They learned how important it was to form partnerships and cooperate with others.

This interaction had enormously positive effects. Players experienced how they could make the (virtual) world a better place through their own actions. When this effect was transferred to the real world, optimism and hope triumphed. Many of the challenges facing the world today could be tackled in a playful way. This was a key to success, because rather than being forced, people were keen to do something of their own accord while having fun at the same time.

A future that became worth living in and even better

than the past – thanks to games. That sounded a little too gonzo for Christiana. The effect of games had been discussed many times before. She had read a very interesting book about it some time ago and could relate to passages in it often. Games and the challenge of winning was something she loved. But what challenges did life hold for her in the future?

19

The thought wouldn't let go of her the whole next day. Again it was David who seemed to have a sure feeling for the right moment. Just before the end of the conference he sent a message. He had met someone and immediately thought of Christiana. "Tonight, rooftop bar!"

After the hubbub of the last few days, she didn't really feel like partying. But curiosity won out. What surprise did he have up his sleeve today? Since the bar was only a few blocks away from her home, she still had time for a shower; and even fifteen minutes of yoga.

She was always fascinated by how much impact such a short workout could have. A moment ago, she had been exhausted. Now she was in the best of spirits as she closed the door behind her. Outside she sucked in the fresh air of spring. The evening sunshine bathed the streets in warm light. Smiling people strolled on the sidewalks in front of her. Amused, she saw a young woman who seemed to conjure up the summer in flip-flops with fake fur. The sense of optimism in the air was infectious.

Christiana could not explain it, but somehow she had the feeling that tonight would be the start of something new. A few moments later she walked through the modern and airy bar towards the roof terrace. A sitting area at the side with cherry blossoms paid tribute to the Japanese spring.

Tempting scents rose to her nose as a waitress balancing plates full of different dishes snaked past her. At the end of the room an elegant, long wooden bar formed the bridge to the roof terrace. The view outside across the surrounding neighborhoods was stunning. The CN Tower dominated the scenery like a lighthouse in the glowing dusk.

Behind two turquoise shimmering small pools David waved to her with excitement. He had gotten hold of a cozy sun lounge under a blue roof. Next to him sat a woman with short, copper-red hair, who hugged her warmly. She couldn't be pigeonholed. An aura of professionalism and friendship surrounded her at the same time. The combination of glittering Harley Davidson T-shirt under a blazer and elegant shoes with jeans, made her a girl rocker and businesswoman. Somehow, she looked familiar to Christiana. But she could not recall why.

David whirled Christiana through the air and then waved to his companion. "Alex and you, there is so much you two have in common – the evening will be long," he whispered conspiratorially before heading off for cocktails. He was right as usual.

Alex lived in Germany, but worked internationally with various companies and start-ups. "I stand on two feet," she pointed to her legs, laughing. On the one hand, she owned a boutique publishing house that produced hand-picked novels, short stories and feature articles. On the other hand, she ran an innovation agency and supported her clients in strategic business development or designed new concepts to implement technology in a meaningful and sustainable way.

Toronto was one of her popular hot spots and the annual conference a fixed date on her calendar. She combined the visit with various business appointments, as Toronto was an extremely attractive location, especially in the media sector. This time she had talks with some studios and producers she wanted to win over for a film series. For years now the Toronto International Film Festival, held annually in September, was established as one of the most important events in the industry worldwide.

"The town has long been known as ‚Hollywood North'," Alex revealed. Many series producers used the city for scenes that resembled New York or Los Angeles. With the difference that shooting film here was much cheaper.

The Casa Loma in Toronto had been just made for X-Men and Harry Potter. A rusty old pickup truck stood in the distillery; a living reminder that the Blues Brothers had once performed their mischief there. Christiana remembered having seen the vehicle many times without knowing its real meaning.

Also, a popular Netflix series about a young lawyer with a photographic memory and no Harvard degree was largely filmed here. The lead's film partner, the then future Duchess of Sussex, had chosen the city as her second residence. Toronto had received regular royal visits.

As a fan of the series Christiana had seen all the episodes. Surprised, she learned from Alex that the headquarters of the series' fictional law firm – officially in Manhattan – was in reality the Bay-Adelaide Centre in Toronto's financial district. She had walked past it several times without noticing the similarity. So one thing they had in common were stories.

20

The next connection was made when Christiana learned that Alex had started an initiative to foster diversity in the technology industry a few years ago. Alex was able to fall back on a network of female founders that had been set up by a friend of hers. But just like Christiana, Alex saw so many more facets in diversity than the typical partitioning into women and men. That thinking fell far too short.

There were not only two sexes. In addition, innovation thrived far more on different perspectives characterized by cultural and ethnic diversity or age and experience than on old-fashioned thinking. There were many good examples, but they were lost in a haze of hyped unicorns. In the technology industry, the main focus was usually on high scalability and the associated fast-growing profits.

The approach from dishwasher to millionaire seemed square these days. Founders wanted to be successful in record time, take their start-up to the stock exchange or sell it at a high profit to one of the GAFA/FAANG giants. Investors expected record speeds for their return on investment. What was worth one euro today had to be worth a hundred times that amount tomorrow. However, the gap between people with an affinity for technology and those who looked in vain for Moore's Law in fenlands grew wider and wider. The view that focused only on financial profit was short-sighted.

New technologies had an increasing impact on the life of society and the environment. And that's where Alex was going to come in. But not like anti-nuclear activists chained to rails, or aspiring talk masters traveling the world of events. She rather wanted to achieve this by telling positive stories about real role models. They had the power to inspire people in many more ways than bad news. She believed much more in the approach of the little prince than in that of newly rich kings. One of her projects was a concept for a somewhat fictional film series but based on real and inspiring people.

David came back with three exotic-looking cocktails. "Is that a hot pepper in there?" Christiana asked in amazement. "Yes, a jalapeno. Alex likes it hot," chuckled David. "All our projects are named internally after chili peppers," added her new friend with a wink.

As it turned out, appropriately enough, her current project had been codenamed "Jalapeno", and she was in the process of putting together a team. It was about regularly reporting on unusual innovations, as well as emerging trends and bleeding-edge research. Handpicking stories that didn't make the headlines or feature on the most prominent news websites. The focus? How and where technology was being used sustainably for humans, animals and nature, and which initiatives and projects were specifically promoting progress in increasing diversity, inclusion and ethics.

The aim was to inspire readers with stories that summarized the facts in a short, entertaining way to achieve a positive and quantifiable effect. Whether by encouraging private citizens to think about making lifestyle changes or by spurring companies on to develop new, more sustainable solutions. Instead of saying what was wrong, the stories would shed light on all the good work that was already taking place. Though there might have been similar initiatives, Alex knew of none whose focus was so unique.

Christiana couldn't believe it. How did the universe always manage to surprise her like this? Ethics, diversity and technology, packaged in winsome storytelling – these were precisely the things that fascinated her.

21

But there was better still to come. Alex already had two team members on board. Lisa was a creative soul who, along with Alex, would help manage the content. Like Alex, she loved the outdoors and was always on the look-out for exciting new topics. Especially in the fields of sustainability, health and education. After a degree in Literary, Cultural and Media Studies, Lisa had spent 14 years at home and abroad collecting a range of experiences in print, radio and television journalism.

Niall, the second team member, was from Scotland. He and Alex had been collaborating on different projects for more than 10 years. They were an unbeatable duo who complemented one another perfectly: Niall's strengths lay in the field of literature.

With a masters in Translation Studies in his pocket, he had made his mark with a series of translations, among them a diversity novel and several bestselling historical thrillers. As a qualified teacher, he was also interested to see how concepts such as sustainability were increasingly finding their way into the classroom. Alex, meanwhile, was unsurpassed in her understanding of complex, technical subject matter. Together they had already written a spy novel.

Project Black Hungarian was a unique blend of fact and fiction. A fictional framework was overlaid with real-life events from a trans-Alpine electric vehicle rally to create an exciting story that had readers puzzling over the line between fiction and reality. Nearly all the characters were based on participants in the rally – with the exception of the villains.

An additional sprinkling of facts helped weave information on hacking and cybersecurity into the storyline, as well as the fundamentals of electric mobility. The story of former CIA employee Edward Snowden, meanwhile, provided Alex an unexpected pillar of support.

His revelations on the extent of American and British global surveillance and espionage practices made her daily research a breeze. All she had to do was read the pages of the Washington Post or The Guardian. The Snowden scandal had broken after she'd already decided to write a spy thriller, but the years had shown that the book's imagined element wasn't so very wide of the mark. The diesel scandal, the car companies' "cartel", the Koch brother funded campaign against electric vehicles, all this came to light post publication.

The novel's hero, who learned of his role shortly before the book appeared, was so inspired by his fictional self that he converted a car into an EV using the latest high-end technology and set a new world record for distance covered on a single charge.

Where "Jalapeno" was concerned, Niall would be the "transcreator" of the English texts. But there was still no one responsible for the strategic planning and long-term development of the project. Alex was a straight talker. Not pushy, just open and honest. She looked Christiana in the eye. "Is that something you'd be interested in?" Christiana was speechless.

Was this the chance she had been waiting for?

EPILOG

In the weeks that followed, Christiana held intense conversations with Alex about the opportunities that "Jalapeno" presented. The offer was more than attractive. Together they decided that Christiana would provide support for a few hours a week during her sabbatical, with a final decision on her involvement pending.

In the meantime, the project had an official name which had been registered as a trademark. Alex had thought long and hard about it. Since she loved wordplay, she had eventually gone for "Chillipicks." Chillies lent spice to a dish, making it more delicate or extra hot. Just like technology, which, depending on how it was applied, could make things easier or more difficult to understand.

Research had shown that chillies were healthy too. Capsaicin, the ingredient that gave chillies their characteristic heat, was not only an anti-inflammatory and natural regulator of blood sugar, but also provided defense against free radicals and reduced the risk of cancer. In a figurative sense, the handpicked positive topics offered readers food for thought. Inspirational appetizers, like canapés served at a friend's cocktail party.

Naturally, tastes were different, and not all topics would be read by everyone. From experience Alex knew that within milliseconds of receiving information, the brain subconsciously took preliminary decisions based on longstanding patterns.

Most of these patterns originated in childhood and were shaped by our upbringing and experiences in an educational or social context. The result was pre-conceived ideas that didn't stand up to serious scrutiny. Or generalizations that barely scratched the surface of a topic.

Such considerations were enormously important for the way in which the articles were written, so Alex developed a new method of storytelling. The central question was how to outflank the brain's subconscious. How to make people read an article without their subconscious supplying its own pre-existing judgments and causing them to skip the information inside?

Alex had a friend who loved bananas. He ate two a day, minimum. Artificial intelligence, however, he saw as a threat to human existence. Perhaps an article about an image-based system that used artificial intelligence to check banana trees for pests, and then presented its findings to farmers, might soften his stance and help win him round? So long as the AI was being used for good and sustainable ends.

Christiana was intrigued to see how the subconscious could be finessed. But for Alex the solution was obvious.

The headline and introductory sentence couldn't reveal the topic. In fact, the headline was intended to rouse readers' curiosity, and the best way to do this was through wordplay. To increase the likelihood that articles would be read in their entirety, Alex limited the word count to 120 maximum.

The figure had been derived from the fact that average reading speed was around 150-200 words per minute. For some, the rate was more like 400-600, but they were the exception. The newsletter, which comprised 5-6 individual topics, could thus be read in 5 minutes. Roughly the time it took to feast on a plate of finger food.

The specifications for headline and length made writing

a challenge as all relevant facts had to be included. There was no space for padding, and yet the text had to be both easy to read and understand. For topics that dealt with technology, this was particularly important.

First, the storytelling concept was put to a focus group. Readers of all ages came from various fields and had a wide range of interests. Based on the first editions, survey results were highly encouraging. 90% of readers loved the approach, were enthusiastic about the subject matter, and said they would recommend Chillipicks to others.

Meanwhile, Christiana's time in Toronto was coming to an end. As much as she enjoyed working on the project with Alex, she realized there was something that lay closer to her heart. Something that affected her personally.

The public at large was completely unfamiliar with the concept of statelessness, even though millions of people worldwide officially had no nationality. All stateless people encountered challenges that those with valid passports wouldn't recognize. Christiana wanted to build a community in which those affected could exchange information and obtain help from allies in the face of difficulty. Alex understood completely – even if she'd have loved to have Christiana on board.

Back in Munich Christiana began implementing her idea in practice, having received her first fellowship grant. All the while, she kept an eye on how things with Chillipicks were progressing.

Since the official launch, the number of readers had risen steadily. 50% regularly read the "inspirational appetizers" that were sent out on Fridays at the same time each week. If the open rates were anything to go by, some read the contents the moment the email dropped. Reader interest and loyalty were twice as high as the international average for newsletters.

Time and again, Christiana wondered at the topics Alex, Lisa and Niall managed to unearth. It was encouraging to see how many people worldwide were committed to concepts like sustainability, diversity and ethics, developing solutions for a fail-safe and fair future.

The information presented wasn't just interesting for private citizens either. It also helped companies develop their business strategies at the same time as doing something good for society and the planet.

That was why, parallel to the weekly editions, Alex had begun populating a knowledge database for corporate clients. Because innovation didn't always mean reinventing the wheel. Indeed, more often than not existing solutions or products could be combined to create something new. Or an idea applied to a different sector or industry. Transposition, it was called in music.

By collaborating with the startups, initiatives and organizations whose work Alex and the team covered in their newsletter, companies could save themselves not just time but development costs. They could also provide financial support for research projects so that these were market-ready and available for use sooner. Not only that.

There was enormous potential for companies to position themselves as attractive employers. Shortages in skilled workers along with increasing digitization further intensified the importance of employer branding and talent management. More and more people valued sustainability, diversity and ethics, and wanted to attribute meaning to their life and work.

Especially the younger generation, those born around the turn of the millennium. For many of them, life wasn't about climbing the ladder and drawing a fat check. Achieving a balance between, or even a way to blend, work and leisure, finding an employer that valued sustainability or social engagement, these things counted for much more.

Likewise, honesty and openness had to be ingrained in company culture. It was equally vital that people of all ages, from the LGBTIQ+ or disabled communities as well as those from different cultural groups were respected and integrated both in the team and by leadership. Everyone should be granted equal opportunities.

One day Christiana was presented with an unexpected opportunity. Her friends from the TEDxTUM-Team invited her to join them on stage to introduce her idea as part of an official talk. The universe was on her side. Things were going well for Alex, too, as Christiana discovered the next time they spoke.

A new client was working round the clock to incorporate three solutions that had been featured in Chillipicks into their business practices. The pilot project was in full swing at headquarters. Once successfully complete, it would be rolled out at various international locations.

One solution offered anonymous assistance to employees experiencing mental health challenges, whether these occurred during or outside of work. A second provided those on the autism spectrum with a special place to take a comforting time-out in the event of overstimulation, while the third allowed people with limited mobility to navigate journeys to and from company sites with ease.

Surveys conducted among job seekers had shown that mentioning the pilot project had a clear positive impact on prospective employees' perception of the firm. It also showed the client that collaborating with smaller organizations meant more could be achieved in less time.

And it wasn't just the world of business that Alex had in her sights. She was convinced that a lasting influence could be brought to bear through online gaming and film. Which was why she would soon find herself back in Toronto.

When Christiana heard she reflected on her time in the city, and on everything that had happened since. A combination of different grants, network contacts and a whole lot of hard work meant she had been able to build her community and recruit her own team.

State.free was officially online and growing. Major newspapers were writing about her and even a career in politics seemed possible. She wondered what the future might still have in store for herself and Alex.

As Christiana waited for her next interview she read the latest Chillipicks. One of the stories instantly sparked an idea.

Another chance.

ACKNOWLEDGEMENT

My sincere thanks go to the people who shared their knowledge with me and supported with time and advice:

Christiana Bukalo, whom I met as part of the TEDxTUM team a few years ago and immediately took into my heart with her cheerful nature. Her project *State.free* and her drive to support people who are stateless like her are inspiring.

David Asabina, whom our mutual friend Raymond introduced me to and who deeply impressed me with his profound knowledge of embedded systems, machine learning and artificial intelligence, and his warm personality.

Marie Helou-Twafik for her fascinating insights on how marketing and eCommerce techniques can be used to support the charity sector.

Hamoun Karami for sharing his vision and efforts on smarter, sustainable waste recycling and making the pirate ship ride an even more memorable experience.

Niall Sellar for his beautiful art of translation and inexhaustible understanding of my stubbornness. Our first meeting at the Urban Angel will remain unforgotten.

Heike and Gerhard for their admirable patience in test-reading the first versions, their valuable tips and their unshakeable belief in my ideas.

The Websummit team for the chance to participate in the Collision Conference as a journalist and speaker and thus allowing me to have special experiences that have been incorporated into the story.

To the many people in Toronto who I met during my research and who made me feel immediately welcome with their candid cordiality.

ALSO PUBLISHED BY CAPSCOVIL

PROJECT BLACK HUNGARIAN

Niall MacRoslin - Alice N. York

Spy Novel

They are young and free. Nils and Hendrik land the perfect job: a secret mission in Switzerland. Pure thrills, expenses all inclusive.

Their target: a revolutionary invention for cars that is to be tested under cover during a 10-day rally across the Alps. A mistake claims the first victims, the ruthlessness increases.

Because their employer - the „Board for Industrial Research and Development" - has been influencing all important political decisions in the market since 1929. And they want it to stay that way. No one has heard of BIRD, no one knows the team. They are effective, secretive and professional. And they work under the protective cloak of an international consulting firm.

Nils and Hendrik learn one thing the hard way: spying is not for rookies!

„*A modern, fresh and fast-moving thriller...totally (and perhaps disturbingly) believable with twists and turns from beginning to end.*"
– Mike Parris, Industry Expert

ISBN 978-3-942358-43-9

GAME - FAINT SIGNALS

Alice N. York

Diversity Novel

Alex leads a thoroughly contented life. In Sandro she has found the right man, and the new job in the solar energy industry seems tailor-made for her.

Driven and experienced, she takes on the management position: an exciting game that she plays to win. It is not the paycheck that drives her, but the recognition, the affirmation; the private smile that says: „Yes, I can".

In addition, business trips to globally operating clients offer Alex an insight into different cultures, taking her to fascinating cities along the way. The job is like a dream come true and serves as the perfect complement to her private life.

Until her world is turned upside down.

Until the rules change, and the world turns ruthless

„*This is a novel that deserves to be read. York has succeeded in creating a heroine whose arc is worth following right through to the bittersweet end.*" - Ebersberger Zeitung

ISBN 978-3-942358-08-8

THE LAST ITERATION OF DEXTER MAXWELL

Matthew Hart

Book #1 of „The Last Iteration“ Science Fiction Series

Dex knows first-hand how tough it is to live on the edge of a thoroughly technologized civilization in Grenver, Colorado. But it also has its perks.

With his small league of street-smart outcasts, he's snarled the system with some of the most brazen stunts of the 22nd century. Not bad for an orphaned sewer rat that can't remember his childhood and will most likely end up iced for ages like any other criminal.

But after a botched stunt, Dex wakes up a foreigner in a brutal, bizarre underground city controlled by more than one shameless force—blind, a sword strapped to his back, and an old man telling him he's the vital component of the coming revolution.

Dex can barely take in the reality of a new time before he's on the run, hunted by vicious assassins, and mixed up in a deadly plot a millennium in the making—and with the fate of two worlds at stake.

"*A mind-bending thrill-ride, Hart has given us a gritty and fascinating vision of the future.*" - Brian David Johnson, Futurist

ISBN 978-3-942358-30-9

SECOND HARVEST

Matthew Hart

Book #2 of „The Last Iteration" Science Fiction Series

Faced with the cold brutality of Ashion the Dark and his thugs, Dexter Maxwell did something no time shifter had ever done before: he traveled back in time permanently.

Now he must live the same thirty days again. But with Ashion and the local warlord hunting him, will there be enough time to save his new – and old – friends?

The clock is ticking. The Ruling Families of Venus have set the Second Harvest in motion. As their chilling plan unfolds, four hundred years of betrayals put Dexter and Ashion on a deadly collision course…and unlock an ancient threat to civilization.

„Matthew Hart excels at combining adventurous science fiction seasoned with sustainability with extrapolated technology developments. The question really is: will descendants of today's billionaires become the ruling families of the future?" – Alice N. York, Author

ISBN 978-3-942358-37-8

www.ingramcontent.com/pod-product-compliance
Lightning Source LLC
La Vergne TN
LVHW091344190726
843491LV00002B/874

* 9 7 8 3 9 4 2 3 5 8 6 2 0 *